FIRST INK

AMY L. GALE

Copyright © 2017 Amy L. Gale

Cover Art by Viola Estrella Author Photo by Guy Cali and Associates, Inc.
All rights reserved. This book or any portion thereof may not be reproduced or used in any manner whatsoever without written permission of the publisher except for the use of brief quotations in a book review. This is a work of fiction. Any resemblance to real characters, places or events is strictly coincidental.

ACKNOWLEDGMENTS

I am enormously indebted to many wonderful people who have helped in my journey to publication of First Ink.

Chris Gale, my husband who inspires and supports me in everything I do.

Carol Riccetti, my mother, who truly believes I can do anything.

Olivia Howe, my P.A., webmaster, social media guru, street team manager, graphic designer, inspirational coach, and friend. I truly believe you are my long lost little sister and I'm so lucky to have such a great friend, fan, fellow author, and promotional wizard with excellent taste in music.

Cindy Davis, my editor extraordinaire who taught me so much in the last few months. You make my work shine and always go the extra mile to help me.

Nicole Gaylord, my proofreader, co-worker, reviewer, and fan. Thank you so much for supporting my work and always offering to lend your eyes.

Viola Estrella from Estrella Cover Art who created my beautiful cover.

Rachel, Sharon and Kelly a.k.a. 'Girls Book Club' who are a great group of friends that constantly support and encourage me. Thank you all so much!

First Ink
A novel

By:

Amy L. Gale

1

VIRGINS

"I can't believe I'm letting him stick that thing in me." A woman's voice echoes over the buzzing.

Not the first time I've heard that line, hell, not even the tenth. Never gets old. I drop my pen and shift my gaze to the door. Three girls, probably in their early twenties, huddle around a notebook, staring at the paper as if the meaning of life is written on the page.

"Listen, Cassie. After waiting six months for an appointment, he can stick whatever he wants in you." A cute brunette who could be a dead ringer for Natalie Portman nudges the blonde next to her. "These guys are the best in the Tri-state area."

Alright, now she's got my attention. Only two years running and Steele Ink is now harder to get into than a virgin's pants. I roll my chair back, leaving the Japanese dragon drawing I've been working on for the past few hours on my desk. "Can I help you girls?"

Six eyes stare at me in unison. The blonde in the middle steps forward, notebook first. Let me guess, a custom design unlike anything the world has ever seen. When you're tattooing in a college town, more clients pick something off the flash wall. I gotta give them dibs for going with their own artwork. As long as they're sober enough to know the ink is permanent, I'll hook them up. I stare at her breasts, unable to pull my eyes away from the double D's peeking out from her V-neck T-shirt. A memory from the blonde who woke up in my bed last night sweeps through my mind, Theresa...or was it Tara? Doesn't matter, we both knew when she walked out the door she wouldn't be coming back.

"We want to get this." The blonde hands me the notebook and takes a step back to her friends like they're attached at the hip.

I focus on the small drawing. A butterfly and three hearts. Really? I do about twenty of these a day. I nod. "Sure, I can hook you up."

The two brunettes standing at her sides move at me like a firing squad. "We have appointments. It's under Cassie Spencer, Jules Brown, and Hailey Matthews," the Natalie Portman lookalike says. "I'm Jules."

My partner, Tito, flips through the computer screen. If he wasn't tattooing, he'd probably work for Microsoft or another tech company as some corporate slave. Suits can't overlook the sleeve of tattoos on both arms. He runs a hand over his tan bald head. "Yep, Cassie's with me. Jules, my apprentice Nick will carve you up. Does everyone know what they're getting?"

The blonde walks toward Tito, her tits bouncing with every step. "Hey Tito, I'm Cassie, and we're all getting the same tattoo."

"Yeah, we're sorority sisters, and we graduate next month. We wanted something to bond us forever." Jules follows Nick to his chair.

"Jules, I promise your tattoo will rock." Nick ties his long brown hair into a man-bun.

Jules just about falls over. What the hell is it with the hair?

Girls are ready to drop their pants when they see him twist that mop on top of his head.

I check out the brunette left standing that has yet to mutter a word. Her skinny jeans stick like glue to legs that go for miles. Hot body, sexy but doesn't know it, and a face more flawless than any pin-up girl I could draw. Who knows, maybe I'll be waking up to those green eyes tomorrow morning. Or at least watch that sweet ass walk out of my bedroom tonight.

She sweeps her long brown locks over a shoulder and stares at me with those please-don't-hurt-me eyes.

Jesus Christ, she's scared shitless. Time to turn on the charm; who knows maybe it'll pay off. "I'm Vic Steele and you're mine."

She drops her hand and holds it out to shake mine. "I'm Hailey Matthews." Her arm trembles. "My first tattoo, go gentle on me." She flashes a meek smile.

I take her hand and lead her to my chair. Her soft skin feels like silk. "Don't worry, I know how to handle a woman."

She blushes and tightens her grip on my hand. "I trust you."

Ugh, like a bullet to the brain. Every time those words fall off a girl's lips it's a recipe for disaster. There should be a neon sign flashing above me saying *I'm not that guy*. I'm all about a good time, nothing complicated.

She takes a deep breath and slowly exhales.

"I won't hurt you...promise."

What the fuck am I saying? Jesus Christ, it's like this chick infiltrated my brain. I mean, I've said shit like this when I want to get in someone's pants but not to get them in my tattoo chair. Maybe I drank too much last night.

We head over to the back of the shop, my domain. The one request I made when I opened the shop with Tito, I need my own space...my own private island. No distractions...except for this girl. What's with this chick?

I gesture toward my chair. "Have a seat."

She lets go of my hand and props up onto the chair, leaning forward with both palms on the black leather. "How do you want me?"

A million thoughts rush through my mind, all of them involving skin to skin contact. "Where do you want me to put it?" Usually that phrase stays in my head when I'm with a woman like Hailey.

She lifts her eyes, locking them with mine. "My right hip. Should I take off my pants?"

How the hell does she think I'm going get the tattoo on her skin if she doesn't? Her pants are sexy as hell but not tattoo friendly. She's either leaving the shop in her underwear or staying here with me, once I get in them.

"Yeah, I need to prep the skin. Any specific colors you want in the design?"

She unbuttons her pants. "No, whatever you think will look best."

My jeans suddenly tighten as she slides down her pants, exposing electric blue underwear. Normally I'd curse under my breath about women who complain about being viewed as sex objects but use their bodies to bring us to our knees every damn chance they get. Hailey's the ultimate tease right now with the innocence of a virgin on prom night. Weird, like she doesn't know she's smokin' hot. I'd be tapping that every second of the day, or at least trying to. College boys aren't as smart as they think if they're letting that piece of tail get away. She has no clue what she does to guys. Her skin glistens under the bright lights. Perfectly pure skin, not a blemish or mark; a tattoo artist's dream. I sit on my stool, trying to calm down before my zipper rips open.

Alright Vic, time to shine. I pull on a pair of black rubber gloves even though I want to touch her, to run my hands from her hip to her thigh, slowly making my way down until she's begging for more. Bet she's never been with a guy like me, yet.

She breathes heavy, gripping the arms of the tattoo chair like it's the only thing to save her from the apocalypse. I spray a gauze cloth with alcohol. She closes her eyes and leans back in the chair. *Dammit*, I'm losing her.

"Just alcohol." I stare at her face, willing her eyes to open.

She nods and slowly lifts her lids. "I'm just a little nervous."

"Don't be. I'm pretty good with my hands." I wink. That line works wonders in a variety of situations. The first time I walked into a shop trying for an apprenticeship, the first time I scored with a client, hell even the first time a girl let me tattoo her when I had no clue what I was doing. Magic words.

I swipe the cloth against her hot skin, slowly dragging it down toward her thigh. Goosebumps follow the path of my hand. The aroma of her fruity perfume blocks out the pungent alcohol. I lean forward, trying to take it all in.

She turns toward me watching every move like I'm about to operate. Pretty much what's happening, I'm about to scar her with an image for life. She nibbles her lip, looking up at me with doe eyes.

I toss the cloth and roll my stool closer to her. "Now I draw the image on your skin. I find freehand drawings more natural. You ready?"

Her tongue darts out of her mouth and runs along her lips. "Yeah."

Her wet lips sparkle under the fluorescent light. My heart speeds like those lips are wrapped around me sending me floating into oblivion. I blink repeatedly and jolt back to reality. Right, the tattoo.

I grab my purple marker with one hand and hold her skin with the other. She flinches and tenses her muscles. I let it go.

Sometimes it's easier to draw on a tensed muscle. I swipe the ink along her hip, forming the lines into the design her friend drew up. It's not like I'm painting the Sistine Chapel but I want it perfect for Hailey. Something that reminds her of me every time her eyes sweep over the ink.

What the hell is with me tonight? I've banged girls way hotter than her. Maybe I'm working too many hours and my brain is fried.

I roll the stool backward and drop the marker on my tray. "How's it look?"

She flashes a small smile and tilts to the side, checking out the drawing. Her face lights up the room. "Amazing. Guess the rumors are true."

"Really? Which ones?" God knows what she's heard about me. Girls talk, and if the ones who attended the one-night-only Vic Steele show after-hours talk around campus I've got the reputation of Gene Simmons after a bottle of Viagra.

"You're the best. Hands down." She locks eyes with me.

Normally I'd follow that up with a sexual innuendo but the way she looks at me, with those clear green eyes full of innocence and trust...I can't do it even though I want to bang her into next week.

"You're about to see how good it gets." Okay, she can take it how she wants.

I set up some small cups and fill them with different colored ink. She watches my every move, like she's memorizing the steps. Is she planning on selling my secrets to the competition? Sadly, no artists around here come close to anyone in this shop. Don't get me wrong, being the best rocks but a little competition is fun sometimes.

I dip my tattoo gun in black ink to get started on the outline. She breaks out into a frenzy of shivers, like someone just blasted her with arctic air. Great. Shaking does wonders for line work.

I place my hand on her hip, trying to steady her. "Nothing worse than a cat scratch."

"I've had cats all my life and when they scratch it hurts like hell." She places a death grip on the arms of the chair.

"Catching yourself with a sewing needle?" I shrug.

She shakes her head. "Nope, that's worse... How about getting a paper cut."

I jerk my head back. "Are you insane, those things hurt worse than getting stabbed."

She relaxes her muscle and chuckles. "Okay, we'll just say it feels like getting a tattoo, nothing else like it."

I nod. "Sounds like a deal. You ready?"

"Can't wait to get your hands on me?" She blushes. "I mean..."

"Just relax, I'll do all the work." If I told her the things I'd like to do to her she'd be out of here and on her way to the police station for a PFA.

She leans back in the chair and takes a deep breath. "I trust you."

The words burn through me with the fire of a thousand hells. I brush it off and hold the skin on her hip tight. The buzz of the gun sounds through the shop, singing sweet music to my ears. I eye the design and press the needle to her skin.

She gasps and lets out a low moan. A split second later, she goes completely limp. You've got to be fucking kidding me.

I set the gun on my tray. "Hailey... Hey, not that bad, right?"

No answer. Her head rolls forward like you see in the movies after the homicidal killer sticks a knife through the victim's back. She limps over, falling on top of herself. Shit. I knew I should've paid more attention in C.P.R. class. Maybe if the instructor didn't look like she was ripped off the pages of Playboy magazine I could've concentrated on the steps.

I pull off my gloves and fling them on the table. "Hailey." Not a peep. I tap each side of her chin softly. "Hey, wake up." The only sound is the buzzing of tattoo guns. *God Dammit*. My heart pounds against my chest. What if she has some condition she failed to tell me about and she's going into shock or something? One last try before I call an ambulance.

I spray some alcohol along my index finger and hold it under her nose. She cringes the second she breathes in the pungent odor. Ah ha, we're getting there. She presses her head against the headrest of the leather chair and slowly opens her eyes.

"You okay?" I hover over her.

"You have a business degree from Northern U?" she mutters, almost whispering.

How the hell does she know that? She shifts her gaze to the wall behind me. I turn to find the object of her interest. Jesus, I forgot that was up there. I focus on the framed bachelor's degree hanging on the wall in a black frame. It seems like another lifetime. Five years and no one ever noticed it before. She's probably delirious. Whatever keeps her talking and conscious works for me.

"Yeah. Back from my Wall Street days." I press the back of my hand against her face. Cool and clammy, not a good sign.

Her face instantly flushes. "Tattoos and suits, perfect combination." Her lips upturn into a sweet smile.

Is she trying to be funny, or is this her number one pick-up line? "Best of both worlds." I've only thrown on a suit for weddings and funerals, but the degree comes in handy when you own your own business. Much more to it than slinging ink. I lean back, trying to give her some air. "Do you want me to stop?" Never in the history of the world has any chick told me yes to that question.

She shakes her head. "I'm okay."

"You sure?"

She nods. "Yeah, now that I know what to expect, my nerves are in check...unless you plan on surprising me."

Hmm, I like her when she's teetering on the edge of consciousness. Sexy, but has no clue of all the innuendos she's throwing at me tonight. Or maybe this whole sweet and innocent deal is all an act.

"Okay, here we go. Round two." I take my gun from the tray and dip the needle in some more black ink.

She turns her head toward me, staring at the needle. I hold her skin taut and fire up the tattoo gun. The buzzing starts again. She watches the needle pierce her skin, leaving a small black dot. Her face turns ashen and wobbles forward...again.

I toss the gun back on the tray and lean my arm out. Kind of like my Mom did back in the day when she made a sudden stop while driving and seatbelts weren't a necessity. I catch her before she swings off the side of the chair.

That's it, game over. I've had enough of this shit. No way am I touching her again...at least not with the tattoo gun. With my luck she'll crack her head off the floor and end up with a concussion. Just what I want, to knock out a client and have the reputation of skull crusher. Sad part is, it would probably increase my business. If I want my career to take off to the point where I can open a shop down in Miami I need a squeaky-clean, untarnished, professional reputation.

I jump up from my stool, kicking it so it rolls away from us. No need to give her any obstacles on her way out of the shop. I set her back in the chair, propping her head on the headrest. Hair bunched around a face of porcelain skin, eyes closed, plump lips ready for anything. She looks like a goddamn princess. Hate to break it to her but I'm far from Prince Charming.

I nudge her shoulder. "Hailey...you're done."

"Hmm." She moans.

The sound rips through me like a fire storm. The next time I hear those noises coming from her lips better be when her lips are locked around me. I let out a breath. First, this situation needs to be handled...now.

She slowly opens her eyes, locking them with mine. Silver specks shine through the sea of green, stabbing me like daggers. "It's finished?"

"I am." I take a step back, giving her some breathing room.

She sits up and curls her neck over a shoulder. "Where is it?"

I run my fingers over her hip. She flinches like I just pressed hot embers against her skin. "Right here."

She scrunches her eyes. "I don't see anything."

"It turned out to be two dots." I wipe down her skin with an alcohol soaked cloth.

"You can't be serious." She jumps up from the chair, almost tripping on the jeans fastened to her ankles. She pulls up her jeans. "When do you plan on finishing this?"

"Uh, when needles aren't involved in tattooing." She can't be serious. "You passed out twice. I'm not chancing it again."

She fastens her jeans and runs a hand through her dark curls. "I can't walk around with an unfinished tattoo."

I laugh. "That tattoo was barely started. Not everyone can handle being tattooed."

She puts her hands on her hips. "Are you saying I can't handle you?"

I shrug. Sounds like a challenge to me.

"Let me enlighten you. I can do this. I was just nervous... that's all. Let's try again."

I shake my head. "Sorry, I'm booked."

"I'm sure you can make time for me if you want." She eyes me from head to toe.

Damn right I can. "Sorry."

"This isn't the last you'll see of me."

Now that's more like it. "Hope that's a promise."

She huffs and storms toward the door. "I'll be back," she mutters right before she rushes out the door.

2

INVISIBLE

The door rips open, sending a thunderous roar of heavy wind and persistence through the shop. "Be right with you," I yell over a shoulder. Never fails, whenever I fire up the computer to place an order or browse some porn, someone comes in unexpected.

"No problem, I'll take a seat."

I scrunch my eyebrows. Why does that voice make my skin crawl and burst into flames at the same time? I hit Save and turn toward the leather couch also known as the waiting area.

Hailey crosses her legs as soon as my eyes reach her body. She leans to the side, letting the black mini-skirt rise a few inches until the edge of her black panties shows for a split second. *Damn.* She quickly moves back as if she's dangling what she's got in front of me. Guess I was dead wrong, she knows exactly how to tease a guy.

"Ah, the terminator." I tip my chin in a s'up kind of way.

"What's that supposed to mean?" She stands and pats her skirt.

"I'll be back," I say in my best Arnold Schwarzenegger voice, trying not to crack a smile.

"Funny." She walks toward me, shaking her hips in that bring-me-to-my-knees kind of way. "I'm here to have my tattoo finished. I don't mind waiting if you're busy." She spins around, scanning the empty shop.

"Not gonna happen, honey." I fold my arms across my chest and look down at her.

She pulls her skirt to the side exposing the two dots she's referring to as a tattoo. "I can't walk around like this."

My eyes instantly gravitate to her smooth skin, following the curve of her hip bone. Things would be so much better if she pulled down the rest of her skirt, and laid in my chair; that's how magic really happens.

"I think you look great walking around like that." I wink.

She lowers her eyebrows and pulls her skirt back up. "I want the tattoo I was promised." She puts her hands on her hips and taps her black heel against the tile floor in time with the Imperial March.

I hold up my hands. "Whoa, I make no promises. Not to any woman, especially not in here."

She huffs. "What's it going to take to get my tattoo finished?"

A hundred different scenarios flash through my mind in seconds, all of them involving that skirt on the floor.

"Sorry, can't help ya." I shrug.

Tito walks in from the back room. "I'll do it."

Apparently he heard the whole conversation while he was in the can. Amazing, he couldn't hear shit when I asked him to cover for me when two chicks came in demanding to know if I was seeing anyone else. Of course, I was seeing them both, but the tattoo gun drowned out all sound when I asked Tito to say I left for the night. Now he has friggin' supersonic ears.

She holds down her skirt, exposing the two dots. He circles around her like a shark in a feeding frenzy.

No way in hell I'm letting him touch her. "Nope. She's mine."

"What?" she growls through gritted teeth.

God, she's sexy as hell when she's pissed...those flushed cheeks flashing a hit of red, the way her lips pout like she's posing for a porno selfie. Way too much to handle, especially for Tito.

"You heard me. No one touches her in this shop but me." Why do I feel like a wolverine that just pissed all over his food?

Tito does a double-take, then holds up his hands. "Got it, hands off."

"Wait, you can't forbid other tattoo artists from fixing you're mistake." She looks at Tito who shrugs and walks away. "Who the hell do you think you are, Hitler?"

"Whatever turns you on, honey." I take a few steps backwards, eyeing her smoking hot, pissed-as-hell body, and head over to my little island in the back of the shop.

"You are finishing this tattoo," she demands.

Her eyes burn through me. A smile breaks through as I rewind the last few minutes in my brain. A feisty brunette dying for my needle to touch her skin. I adjust my stool, trying to hide the bulge forming in my pants. If she knew how much she was turning me on she'd probably punch me in the face, or slam me in the chair. Either way I'm all for it.

The door opens and closes with a quick swoosh. Finally, she gave up. I turn toward the sound, hoping to get a glimpse of her perfect ass as she walks away. No such luck. A tall guy with shoulder length hair grabs a tattoo album from the table. He plops down next to Hailey.

"Waiting for Hitler?" She looks over his shoulder as he flips the page.

"Huh?" The guy eyes her, a shit-eating grin plastered on his face.

No fucking way I'm letting him have her. "Hey, you need help, man?"

"Yeah, I've got a 4:30 with Tito."

Tito swings around the corner like he's a friggin' fireman sliding down the pole. "I'm all set. Just finished the sketch."

The guy runs a hand through his hair and stands up. "Maybe I'll see you when I'm done." He scans Hailey's body from head to toe.

Is this guy for fucking real? "She won't be here."

"I'll leave once my tattoo is finished." She grabs a photo portfolio and leans back on the couch, flipping through the pages like she's reading some chick magazine.

My tattoo gun won't touch her skin again. Next time she might smash her head on the floor...or worse. Not worth it, for either one of us. She'll get sick of this game soon.

I plop on the couch next to her, taking the last guy's place. "Are you seriously going to sit here until we close?"

She crosses her legs, swinging her black heel around in a circle. "Yep, unless you finish the tattoo, then you'll be rid of me." She flips through the pages, not even turning her head to look at me.

I lean over closer. "Maybe I don't want to get rid of you." That'll shake up this ridiculous game she's playing.

She stops, frozen. Like she just heard something she never thought possible. She turns her head toward me, moving closer so our lips almost touch. "Maybe I don't want to leave."

She wants more than a tattoo. Am I slipping? I should've seen this coming a mile away. I move forward, ready to give her the full Vic Steele experience.

She jolts her head back a split second before our lips touch. "Let's keep it professional. I'm here for your artwork, not your other talents."

I let out the deep breath I didn't realize I'd been holding. *God dammit*, she's a siren in an innocent school girl's body. Why the hell does she drive me insane? I need her, and if the only way to get that skirt off her is to tattoo her again, maybe I should just do it.

No way. Come on, Vic. Stop thinking with your dick and let a little blood flow back to your brain. Who the hell does she think she is? I invented this game. There's no way in hell I'm going to lose.

"You can't handle my talents…none of them." I lean over her shoulder, my breath blowing a few strands of her hair against her neck.

She fidgets and a line of goosebumps erupt along her skin. "I doubt that." She leafs through a portfolio.

I stand up and point to the Japanese dragon gracing the open page. "That tattoo is a custom sketch. Won me the cover of Ink Magazine last year." I take a few steps away, toward my chair. "More talent than you can imagine, with or without ink." I wink and walk away.

Her volcanic stare shoots through my chest. I head over to my sketch table and plop into the leather seat, adjusting myself so I can see her from the corner of my eye. She slams the sketchbook closed and sets it back on the table.

Huh, I guess I got someone's panties in a bunch. Not the first time, and it sure as hell won't be the last. I smirk.

She trots to the other side of the shop. What the hell is she doing? Does she plan on tattooing herself? This chick is crazy.

I stare, my eyes glued to her every move. She struts to Tito's chair, leaning forward until I can see the black hem of her underwear. *Damn.* I picture her bent over the chair, slamming myself into her as she screams my name. Who knows, if she plays her cards right it might happen.

She nods her head as Tito wipes off excess ink from the guy's tattoo. "Looks great. Maybe the talent's all right here." She turns toward me, flashing a sexy half-smile.

Yeah, real funny. I rush toward them like a freight train on nitrous. Tito's a good tattoo artist, hell he might even be great, but he's not Vic Steele. Never was and never will be. I've worked my ass off to make the cleanest lines and images that pop off your skin, like they're real. Unless Tito had divine intervention, she's doing this shit to get a rise out of me, and not the kind I'm used to having.

"Sweet tat, Tito." I do a quick once-over his work.

"Thanks man, Evan here is sitting like a rock." Tito adds midnight blue to his palate. "Two more hours and this dragon will breathe fire."

Jesus Christ, I have to deal with this chick flirting with straggly haired Evan while she blows sunshine up Tito's ass? Not my idea of a productive day. I run a hand through my hair and blow air out my cheeks. "Catch you guys later, I have a killer eagle tat in five."

"Wait, you're tattooing someone else?" Hailey scrunches her eyebrows and stares at me, the same way my mom's golden retriever does when she can't understand why I won't play ball in the middle of a snowstorm.

"Yep. They made this thing called an appointment about six months ago." I head over to my station and grab the sketch of the design.

She follows me like a moth to a flame. "You could've finished this tattoo if you just started when I walked in here."

I get ready for the next client like she's not standing so close her fruity perfume burns through me. "Yeah, probably."

"You know what, Vic? You might be this amazing tattoo artist, but as a human being you're a real asshole." She turns around and storms toward the door.

"Whoa, I think you got it all wrong, babe. I am not tattooing you because I'm afraid you're gonna pass out for a third time, and probably smash your head off the floor or something. I'm pretty much protecting you from yourself. You should probably be thanking me, you know, like I'm your hero."

She huffs and breaks into a demented smile. "You're a real piece of work, you know that?"

Damn, her hatred for me at this moment makes me want to throw her down on that leather couch and show her just how bad she wants me to finish. I set up a few small cups for my color scheme. "That's what I hear." The fire in her eyes floats through the room like a raging inferno. Life lesson, don't try to outsmart a player. College doesn't prepare you for times like this.

She storms toward the door, looking over her shoulder. "First of all, you're sure as hell no hero, and second, I am not your babe." She holds up her fingers, making air-quotations before rushing out of the shop.

"Not yet." I stare as she dashes out of the shop, her hair swinging like a wrecking ball. Why do I want her to come back?

3

TIME WARP

"Thanks for letting me crash at your place for the weekend." My brother Sam catches the keys to my apartment as I push open the door to the shop.

"Don't drink all my beer." I give him a quick nod and head inside.

I might drop dead if my little bro actually called instead of showing up like he's stranded. I get it; he wants some time away from his home in our parents' basement. Newsflash, if he gets an actual job, he can move the hell out. Or even find a place here in the city, even though it's more like a glorified town. I get it, he's got dreams...been there. Maybe his band will make it and he'll be a golden guitar god. Gets tons of ass with the gig either way. He probably has some chick waiting on the steps already. Guess the genetics shine through.

I file across the shop, balancing the portfolios I was updating last night, along with a cup of coffee. I set everything down on the table near my station. Okay, one two-hour session of a photo realistic timber wolf, and then a quick ankle rose for a college chic. I might even have some time for a walk-in today.

Heels click along the floor forming an angry melody. I turn

and glance from the corner of my eye. A smokin' hot body invades my field of vision. She arranges the portfolios on the table, angling them like Martha Stewart is about to critique her work. What the hell is going on? Did Tito hire someone without telling me?

I spin my chair around and lock eyes with the vixen who's quickly become my nemesis. "Ah, the terminator returns."

"Hail, Hitler." She continues to arrange some flyers next to the portfolio, shoving her ass in my direction.

You've got to be fucking kidding me. She's insane. Totally psychotic mixed with sexy as fuck. How the hell did I get dragged into this demented game? Hell, I'll play. Hope she knows the stakes are higher than she thinks. She better be ready to lose big-time.

Tito lifts his chin and smirks, returning to his drawing. *Dick!* He probably hired her just to piss me off. I get it, he's jealous of my skills. Well, he's about to see a whole new set.

"What gives? You the new cleaning lady? I'll hook you up with a French maid costume."

She shoots daggers at me with one look. "Unlike you, I don't want to hang around here like a useless lump until I head to the chair." She finishes arranging her masterpiece.

"Awesome. Free services." I try and hold back a smile.

She walks toward me like a freight train on fire, slamming her hands on her hips and stopping an inch before me. "I can go a block up the road and they'd be thrilled to tattoo me. Especially since it involves fixing a Vic Steele tattoo gone wrong."

I slide a hand in my pocket and nod. "Yeah, but you won't have the Vic Steele tattoo your friends have." Okay, so I didn't tattoo either one of them but she gets the point.

She huffs. "What's it gonna take to get this done?" She drops her hands and flashes those puppy dog eyes at me. "The whole point was to get matching tattoos to always remind us of the sisterhood. Now I'm left with nothing."

"Wow, maybe you should be holding your Oscar and thanking the academy." An involuntary smile graces my face.

She bows her head like she just missed the final pass in the championship game. "It's not like I expect you'd understand."

Tears fill her eyes. *God dammit*. What is it with chicks? It's like they know exactly when to turn on the waterworks and make us feel like shit. I can't let her break down in the shop, it's not good for business.

I lift her chin until her eyes lock with mine. "I've got an easy schedule today." So much for using any extra time to tie up loose ends. Someday I'm actually gonna get enough peace and quiet to add some kick-ass drawings to the mix. "Got dinner plans?"

She shrugs. "Maybe you could fit me in before your next appointment."

"Yeah, like I'm gonna tattoo you when you haven't eaten. You'll probably pass out before you hit the chair. Not gonna happen."

She scrunches her eyebrows like an eternal struggle is going down in her brain. "Okay. Your treat." She heads over to the front counter and clears off the area near the register. "Just so we're clear, this is not a date."

"Hell no. Your payment for all the tidying up around here." I gesture toward the waiting area. It's never looked better. I guess the place needs a woman's touch.

She bites her lip, trying to hold in a smile.

"It's gonna be a few hours. Want me to pick you up at your dorm?"

She stops dead, like time just froze. "Sounds like a date, maybe I should meet you there."

I hold up my hands. "Not a date. More like a business meeting. Who knows, maybe you can convince me to take another shot at that tattoo."

She spins her head around, almost like Regan in the Exorcist. "Hmm, my law elective just might come in handy... Okay, Gunter Hall room 204. What time?"

"Eight. Should I bring flowers?" I wink.

"Yeah, funny." She flings her purse over a shoulder and heads toward the door.

I hold open the door and guide her forward, placing my hand in the small of her back. The aroma of her fruity perfume fills the air. I breathe deep, imagining her hair flowing down her naked back. Her ass propped up as I thrust myself deep inside of her.

She stops and turns back toward me. "I require utensils and a tablecloth."

I stare at her red lips, trying to will my dick to stay down. "No Mickey D's?" I let out a chuckle. "Don't worry, I got you covered. Who knows, you might even have fun."

"With you?" She looks me up and down.

"Don't knock it till you tried it."

We walk side by side down the sidewalk. The lukewarm breeze blows her skirt along her perfect thighs. I resist the urge to run my hand up her leg to her panties. What the hell am I doing? It's like a pity fuck without the fucking. She waves and turns the corner. My eyes glue to every move until she disappears.

I WEAVE my Mustang in between the lines of the tight parking lot and pull into a spot. Jesus Christ, some drunken frat boy better not hit my doors. If that's the case, it'll be their last party. I step out of the car and close the door, clicking the key fob as I slide my wallet into the black dress pants I haven't worn since last year when I was at my cousin's wedding. Two girls stand to the side of a sign that reads Gunther Hall. At least I know I'm in the right place. I give them a quick nod and head toward the door.

"Hey, you coming in?" a blonde wearing shorts up to her ass cheeks yells to me.

"Yeah. Do I need to scan a fingerprint or promise my first born?"

"Not if you're with me." She gestures for me to follow her.

Whoa, if I knew it was this easy to score I'd hang out around here more often. If Sam came with me, these girls would lose their minds. "Thanks."

She presses a few buttons and pulls open the door. "Here to see anyone in particular?" She flutters her eyelashes and nibbles her lip.

"Yeah, looking for room 204." I scan her from head to toe before I can stop myself.

"Up the steps and to the right." She flashes a sexy smile. "I'm in 110 if you get lost or something." She walks away, glancing over her shoulder before she turns the corner.

I stare at her ass bouncing under her shorts. *Damn.* Is every girl in here hot as fuck? Maybe I should nix this dinner and head over to room 110. I mean, Hailey doesn't give a shit about me. She just wants a tattoo, which takes very few skills to pull off. Letting someone else finish it would give them bragging rights, and I can't let that happen. Hell no. No one fixes a Vic Steele tattoo because they're always fucking awesome.

If I finish the tattoo I won't get to see her sweet ass around the shop anymore. Now I get why chicks like to lead you on… prolong the agony, or the ecstasy. Never thought I'd miss being called Hitler every time she sees me. Those fiery eyes filled with passion burn through me like hot coals. Somehow she scarred my soul, like a perfect tattoo. I can't peel my eyes away.

I head up the stairway. She's screwing with me, and it's making me want her more. What the fuck? It's like she's some voodoo master putting her evil spell on me. And now, I'm taking her to dinner with no hope of fucking her after. God, it's like I turned into a priest.

I focus on the numbers on the dark gray doors...204. I hold up my hand to knock a split second before the door swings open.

Hailey stands in the doorway and tugs on her black sundress. Her sexy-as-hell heels make those legs go on for miles. I'm doomed. How do I pry myself away from this alluring creature?

"You're late." She glances at her cell phone screen and drops it in her small purse.

"Had a little moment with the girl from downstairs." I flash a half-smile which turns her cheeks crimson. A little jealousy goes a long way.

"You're a real piece of work. Let me guess, you had a quickie before taking me out. Real classy." She pulls the door shut with way more force than necessary.

She gets under my skin in a million different ways. If I could just get under hers...or any part of her, for that matter. "I thought this wasn't a date."

"It's not." She stomps down the hallway.

"Hmm, then why are your panties in a bunch?" I catch up to her.

She stops right before the steps and spins toward me, her long brown locks smacking me in the face as she moves. "First of all, this is the furthest thing possible from a date. Second, you have absolutely no effect on my panties whatsoever." She grabs the strap of her purse and marches down the steps.

"And third, you're a little jealous of the harem of woman who want me." I hold in a laugh and hop down the steps, trying to catch up with her.

She shakes her head. "You're delusional. And I think those girls should take a trip to the psych floor of the hospital."

"Very unprofessional talk for a business meeting, Hailey." That should set her off into a frenzy.

"Which car is taking me to this meeting, a Benz with a Swastika on it?" She pushes open the door and steps onto the pavement.

Ah, I get it. The Hitler-mobile. "Close, the black Mustang." Her sweet ass has never been nestled in a better machine. I click the key fob.

She struts over to the passenger side door and pulls open the handle. "So, where we going?" She slides into the seat and softly closes the door.

At least she respects my wheels; not likely any of that will flow to me. "How about you stop asking so many questions and let me surprise you." I get in the driver's side and fire up the engine.

"Your surprises are dangerous." She pulls on her seatbelt.

"You have no idea." I slip into Reverse and hightail it out of the parking lot.

She grabs the seatbelt, pulling it over herself like she's about to crash into a mountain. "Am I going to live long enough to eat dinner?"

"Don't worry, she sticks to the road like glue." I stare at the road, catching a glimpse of Hailey out of the corner of my eye.

She nibbles her nails and pushes against the floor mat like she has her own personal brake.

"What's wrong? Can't handle a little speed?" I put my hand on her knee.

She knocks it off with one swoop. "First lesson of driving, keep your hands on the wheel."

I smirk and grip the leather steering wheel. Doesn't feel even remotely as good as her soft, flawless skin.

She pranced around the shop, using her unique tactics to try and get me to tattoo her like a woman on mission. No fear, no regrets, just pure passion charging her to get exactly what she wants. What's gotten into her now? It's like she's reverting to damsel-in-distress mode.

I make a sharp left and pull into the parking lot of the Cedar Point Inn, one of the best restaurants in town.

She lets out the breath she'd been holding as I slide into a parking space. "Really? Didn't think this was your kind of place."

I shrug. "You said utensils and tablecloths required."

I get it…because I like to play the field and tattoo for a living I'm all about the bar scene and have no idea what a real date constitutes. Okay, so I'm rusty in the romance department. Haven't had a steady girl in years but I remember how it works. Besides, I need to focus on my career with no complications. Why the hell am I so worried about this chick's opinion of me?

"I'm impressed." She opens the door and steps outside, sliding one leg over the other like they do in those sexy pantyhose commercials. No way in hell it's a coincidence. She knows exactly what to do and how to do it. Could I have met my match?

"Don't act so surprised." Maybe she's learning there's a hell of a lot more to Vic Steele than meets the eye. Don't get me wrong, I don't mind my reputation. Hell, sometimes I'm the first to brag about it, but not everything is always what it seems.

I hop out of the car and click the fob to lock the doors. She struts along the length of the car and comes around to my side. No spunky remarks or digs at my motives, just a girl on a date with a guy. Oh yeah, a non-date-business-meeting. Why is this sudden change scaring the shit out of me?

"Never been here, and always wanted to try it." She moves forward, stopping about a foot away from me.

Yeah, I'm starting to feel the same way. We walk side by side on the short walk to the stone-faced building. My heart thumps against my chest like the next move will make or break me. Why am I so friggin' nervous? I took out hundreds of chicks, maybe more. But this one, for some god-only-knows-why reason embedded herself in my brain like a tumor. Is she harmless, or will she eat away at me like a cancer?

I place my arm in the small of her back, guiding her through the doorway. She jumps, like electric shocks jolt through her. Maybe she feels it too. I mean, if she could get past the bitter hatred and wishing death upon me. I move closer, breathing in the aroma of her fruity perfume.

She locks her arm with mine. "It's a classy place, we need to look the part."

"I'm not complaining." I flash a half smile. Blood rushes through my veins sending bolts of adrenaline through my body. How the hell am I going to refrain from knocking everything off the table and fucking her into next week?

I take a deep breath to calm my body enough to make it through this dinner. I follow the red carpet to the podium with the most beautiful girl that exists on my arm. "Reservation for Vic Steele."

The hostess runs her fingers along the paper in front of her. "Ah, Mr. Steele. Right this way." She flashes a sexy smile at me and gestures for me to follow her. *Damn*, hot as sin. Too bad I could give a fuck less. My god, am I losing my mind?

Hailey grips my arm tighter. What the hell is happening? Is she jealous the hostess is shooting her fuck-me eyes at me every chance she gets?

The hostess stops at a secluded table in the back. "Enjoy." She grazes her fingertips along my forearm as she walks away.

The dim lit room illuminated by soft lights and candles only fits about fifteen tables inside. Guess that's why it takes forever to get a reservation. Tito banged the hostess a few times and by some miracle, they're still friends. She got me right in. Not sure what this favor will cost me.

I do a once-over, taking in the glow of the crystal chandeliers and gold tablecloths. It's like I stepped into the fucking golden age of Hollywood. Next thing I know, Frank Sinatra steps out from behind a curtain and starts crooning.

"Huh." Hailey grabs the back of the chair.

Dammit. I quickly step over and pull the chair out for her. "What's wrong?"

She sits and shrugs. "I didn't expect a place like this to hire girls like her."

I take a seat and pull in my chair. "Gotta keep the businessmen happy." She has no idea how the world works. People want to see beauty and most guys want to look at a hot piece of ass.

"Is this a front for a brothel or something?" She opens her menu.

"Nah, I'd know about it if it was." Not even close to the right thing to say. If I could talk with my brain instead of my dick, then maybe she wouldn't think of me as a player.

"True. Your reputation precedes you." She closes her menu and sets it down on the table.

"Yeah, for providing awesome ink to my clients." I open my menu but can't peel my eyes away from her. I stare at her red lips glistening as she talks.

"Among other talents." She taps her fingernails on the table.

The waiter steps in before I can say anything else. "Good evening. Are there any questions about the menu?" He fills our water goblets.

I shake my head. Food is food. And at this second, the only thing I want to devour is sitting across from me.

"I'll start with a Grey Goose Martini, extra dirty." She sits back in her chair. "Your treat, right?"

So she's a dirty kind of girl. "Anything you want." I wink. "I'll have a beer. What's on draft?"

"Sir, we carry the finest of imported bottles." The waiter eyes me from head to toe, staring at my forearms sticking out from my half-rolled up sleeves.

Guess the sleeves of tattoos make him think I'm either a brain dead rock star or some thug who came into a few bucks. "Okay, I'll have whatever you think is good. Surprise me."

"Are you sure you wouldn't like to look at the beer list? It's quite extensive." The waiter scrunches his forehead like I asked him to tell me the secret of immortality.

"I trust you, bud." I give him the s'up nod and open my menu.

"Very well. I'll be right back with your drinks." He scurries away.

I look at Hailey over the top of my menu. "First time I'm here. Still learning the ropes."

She nods and takes a sip of her water. "Long way from Mickey D's."

I unbutton the top button of my gray dress shirt. I could never survive in the corporate world. These monkey suit dress shirts suffocate me, kinda like this chick. "I'm not all Big Macs and ink, babe."

She leans forward. "Yeah, you're also a man-whore. I've heard the stories. You're a legend around the campus."

Normally I'd scream *Hell Yeah* to that comment, but I can't stand it when she says shit like that to me. It's like I want to start fresh with her, without her knowing all this shit about me.

"Listen, I'm not a relationship kind of guy. It just complicates everything." I sip my water. "Plus, I don't know how much longer I'll be here."

The waiter brings our drinks. "Are you ready to order?"

She raises an eyebrow, then turns toward the waiter. "I'll have the sea scallops appetizer and the lobster tail stuffed with crab meat as my entrée."

"Very good choices, Madame. And for you sir?" The waiter looks down at me like he's afraid I might pounce on him if he says the wrong thing.

"I'll have the shrimp cocktail and a filet mignon, medium."

"Excellent sir." He takes our menus and leaves in a flash.

"What do you mean? You make it sound like you're dying or something." Her eyes, full of concern, stare at mine.

What's with this sudden interest in my wellbeing? I sip my beer. "Would you miss me?" The strong flavor of hops flows along my tongue. Would it kill them to serve a good old fashioned Miller Lite?

She smirks. "Yeah, like I miss a cold sore after it goes away." She sips her martini.

"So you're telling me you have herpes." I hold in a laugh.

She huffs. "You're an asshole." She leans back in her chair like she can't get away from me fast enough.

"Yeah, but I'm kinda funny." Oh shit, she's probably ready to bolt. I smile, trying to keep her from throwing that $20 martini in my face, and storming out.

A smile bursts through her sexy lips despite her struggle to hold it in.

"I plan on opening a shop in Miami, just as soon as I can. Pretty close to making it happen. I want the world to have the opportunity to get a Vic Steele tattoo."

"Maybe someday I'll have a finished one." She sips her martini and slides her tongue along her top lip.

God, this chick destroys me. I squirm in my seat, adjusting myself so I can keep it in my pants for the rest of the dinner.

"Play your cards right, anything can happen." I raise my

eyebrows. "So, how about you? What's in store for you after graduation?"

"Well, first I want a finished tattoo to match the one my sorority sisters have." She taps her fingernails on her glass. "Then I'm heading to grad school."

"Let me guess, tactics to wear people down until you break them. Like they do with prisoners of war?" I slug my beer.

"Close. Clinical psychology." She gulps down the rest of her drink. "Figuring you out is beyond my skills at the moment."

"Funny." Jesus, she's the perfect mix of cute and sexy-as-hell, with a warped sense of humor like me. Didn't know girls like this existed. "So you want to shrink heads for a living?"

She shrugs. "Maybe. I'm not off to a good start. My ex was cheating on me with his yoga instructor. Didn't see that coming. I guess I need to work on my observation skills."

What asshole would cheat on Hailey? Didn't he get it? He had a hot-as-hell awesome chick and he fucked it up. Moron. I shake my head. "If a guy wants to hide something, he'll cover his tracks like a mass murderer on the run. Not your fault."

She squints her eyebrows and leans forward. "Wow, you actually said something nice. Did aliens take over your brain or something?"

Yeah, or something. "I'm nice." I jerk my head back like she threw porcupine quills at me.

"Uh-huh. If something's in it for you."

Okay, she got me there. The waiter steps in just in time to break the awkward tension. He places our appetizers in front of us.

"*Bon appetite.*" He turns and flows through the room.

Hailey pops a scallop in her mouth. "Don't freak but I'm going to grad school at the University of Miami."

"You're shittin' me." This is way beyond coincidence. It's like the gods want us to be together. First, she shows up in my shop, then refuses to leave, and now she's going to grad school in the city where I'm ready to settle down?

"My god, this is amazing." She shoves the last two scallops in her mouth. "Oh, I should probably tell you, I'm not one of those girls who don't eat. And I plan on having dessert too."

Good, more time I get to spend with her. Wait...what the fuck is wrong with me? She jumped through my hoops, we're out to dinner. I'll finish her tattoo if it kills the both of us. Then we'll be on our way. No need to prolong the inevitable. Maybe I'll see her sometime in Miami, maybe not. But spending any more time than necessary together is bad for the both of us.

The waiter comes back with another round of drinks and our entrees. She sips the martini as soon as the waiter sets it down. "Appetizers were killer. Can't wait to get my hands on this lobster."

Now all of a sudden she's in a feeding frenzy and slamming martinis? Holy fuck, one drink and she's shit-faced. "Want some water?" There's no way I'm taking her back to the shop half-loaded. She'll probably pass out and puke on me at the same time.

"Oh my god, this is better than sex." She eats the lobster stuffed with crabmeat like she hasn't seen a hot meal in weeks. Within five minutes, there's nothing but a shell.

I cut my filet and stab a piece with my fork, shoveling it in my mouth. It melts within seconds. Perfect texture and flavor. *Damn,* best steak I ever had.

"So what do you do for fun? You know, when you're not hanging out in my shop."

She shrugs. "The usual, listen to music, shopping trips with my friends, watch movies...I'm a big Star Wars fan."

I never would have pinned her for a sci-fi nerd. "I'm one with the force."

She giggles. "Yeah, the dark side."

"That's the best one." Ever since I was a kid Darth Vader was my favorite character. Guess I never went for the superhero type. "I never get why they didn't fix the glitch in the first movie...well, the fourth."

She scrunches her forehead. "What are you talking about?"

Ah, I know a little Star Wars trivia. Time to wow her with my brain...not my usual game. "You know, with the Stormtroopers. They're supposed to be clones of Jango Fett."

She sips her martini. "Yeah."

"Well, when C-3PO and R2-D2 are in the control room of the Death Star, the storm troopers barge in and one hits his head on the door. That means they can't be clones, or they would all be the same height."

She nods, holding back a smile. "I never noticed that."

"Bet I just changed your world." I scarf down my meal almost as fast as she devoured that lobster. "This place lives up to the hype."

She raises an eyebrow locking her eyes with mine. "Certainly lives up to the hype." She slugs her martini.

Liquid confidence, or does the truth come out when she's buzzed? "Maybe I'll take you home. I think the martinis got the best of you."

"Umm, it's my second one. I know what I'm doing." She sloshes down the rest of her drink just as the waiter approaches. "Can we please have our bill?"

"Of course. Did you enjoy everything?"

"Yeah, everything was awesome. My compliments to the chef." Wow, I sound like one of those fake idiots who come in asking for a tat of their college mascot or logo, hoping they don't get any stray ink on their business shirts.

"Better than sex...well, maybe not...I guess we'll see."

The waiter's face turns a bright shade of crimson. "Very

happy you enjoyed it." He bolts away faster than the speed of light.

"Classy." I kinda like this side of Hailey. No holding back. Imagine if we could all live life like this. We'd either get our ass kicked on a daily basis, or live a lot longer from not holding everything in.

"It's true. I guess the alcohol loosened me up." She tucks a stray hair behind her ear.

I bet nothing on that hot body is loose. "What now? Want me to take you back to the shop and finish that tat? I think you might be able to handle it now."

She shakes her head. "Not yet, I want to see what else I can handle."

The waiter hands me the check. I throw my credit card at him like it's on fire, without even glancing at the charges.

"I've got Episode IV and a gallon of chocolate marshmallow ice cream…wanna look for the glitch?" I squirm in my seat, trying to hide the bulge in my pants.

Either one of us can Google this in a second and probably watch the exact scene on YouTube. Whatever she says next tells me everything I need to know.

"I'm up for it all." She hops up from her seat just as the waiter returns.

I give him a much higher than necessary tip and grab Hailey's hand, pulling her out of the restaurant like she's going to change her mind in a split second. Okay, so her mind isn't crystal clear but no one in the history of the earth can get annihilated on two martinis. This is my chance to be with the one woman I want more than anything. Will the night last forever or will it disappear with the dawn?

4

THE FORCE IS STRONG IN THIS ONE

How can Hailey turn me into a deranged psycho? I fumble with my house key with one hand, and hold Hailey's with the other, like she's going to take off running if I let her go. Guess I'm channeling my inner Ted Bundy. I am kinda keeping her captive, just not against her will. My copy of Star Wars is on VHS so, other than fast forwarding, scene-skipping doesn't exist. Guess we'll be watching all two and half hours of the movie.

Sam pulls open the door a split second before I put the key in the lock. Jesus, I forgot about Sam. At least he's on his way out. And he sees Hailey so he'll know not to come back anytime soon. One great thing about Sam, he's not a douche. He gets it, and won't fuck things up for me. Best bro in the world.

"Hey." He eyes Hailey and then shifts his gaze toward me, trying to hold in that "nice going" grin.

"Sam, meet Hailey. We're watching Star Wars." I step through the door, pulling Hailey with me."

"Hi Sam." Hailey waves with her free hand as she passes by him in a flash.

"Yeah, hey...wait you're what?" He squints his eyes and looks at me like I just told him I was joining a feminist group. "Whatever. Have fun. See you in the morning, bro." Sam locks the doorknob before walking out.

I get it; he thinks I'm playing the Princess Leia in the gold bikini card. No way in hell Hailey would go for that one.

"Prepare to be amazed." I kneel in front of the TV and dig through a mess of VHS and DVD's scattered on a glass shelf of the TV stand. Yes, the gods are on my side. I pull out Star Wars: A New Hope like it's the Golden Fleece.

"Umm. Yeah, I'm pretty amazed those still exist." She sits next to me. "Are you going to pull out an eight-track next?"

"Not till the second date." I wink.

Her face turns crimson. "Our second date better be you fixing my tattoo."

"I thought this wasn't a date." I smirk and pop the video into the VCR. "Are you asking me out?"

Her eyes widen. She nibbles on her lip more like she's trying to hold back a smile. She feels it too. That energy that exists between us, like wind to a fire. A little gust makes the flame rise to the heavens. Exactly what she does to me.

"I'm in." I stand up and hold out my hand.

Her hand shakes as she slides her fingers into mine. I help her up and lead her toward the green leather couch across from the TV. Thank God Sam cleaned up before heading out. The aroma of stale cigarettes still lingers but the lemon air freshener he stuck on the end table cuts down on the corner bar smell and gives off the bachelor pad vibe. Guess he was hoping to get lucky tonight. I'll make it up to him.

I take a seat on the couch and fiddle with the remote. If this damn video doesn't play I better renew my Netflix membership before she leaves. There's no way in hell I'm letting her walk out on me until this second date is set in stone...or ink. Whatever works.

She plops down on the couch next to me and glances around the living room, shifting her eyes from the vintage framed Led Zeppelin poster to the dragon I sketched along the back wall, breathing fire into the archway to the kitchen.

"Is that yours?" She sets her hand on my knee.

I look down at her red fingernails draped on my leg. She catches herself and quickly pulls away. Why is she fighting this so much? It's like her brain won't let her body succumb to the power of Vic Steele. Guess I better find a way to turn off her brain.

"Yep, took me a month and a half but you're looking at original artwork from yours truly." I lean back and put my arm around the top of the couch, slowly draping it along her shoulder.

She stays still, unable to pull away. "It's amazing. I guess you do live up to the hype."

"Hmm. Is that a compliment?" I put my hand over her forehead.

She giggles. "Yeah, I must be delirious."

I slowly slide my hand down her cheek, brushing my thumb across her lip. Her eyes lock with mine. I lean forward and slowly press my lips against hers. My heart races like John Bonham's playing a drum solo in my chest. I gotta take it slow, or she'll bolt out of here in a second. She lets out a slight moan as my tongue slides around hers.

She lunges forward, wrapping her arms around my neck and weaving her hands in my hair. Holy shit, did hell just freeze over? Maybe I got her all wrong. I move my hands down to her hips and lift her onto my lap, so she's straddling me. I lean back, pressing myself against her thin panties, letting her know exactly how bad I want her. She's probably going to stop cold turkey and leave me high and dry. Probably all part of her master plan to fuck with me as much as humanly possible. Not sure why she gets off on aggravating the piss out of me, but I'll ride this train until it crashes and burns.

I slip my hands underneath her sundress and slowly move them up to her breasts. Ah, no bra, nice. I run my thumbs along her rock-hard nipples. She breathes heavy and presses down on me, slowly rocking back and forth. Jesus Christ, this is really happening.

I glide my hands around to her back and hold her tight, lifting her for a split second. She wraps her legs around me letting out a low moan. No way this is the martinis; she wants me as much as I want her. I slowly turn and ease her down on the couch.

I pull away for a split second and look into the bright green eyes staring at me, filled with a mix of passion and fear. I can't be a dick, not to her. Believe me, I want her more than I've ever wanted a girl lying on my couch. Does she want me…I mean really want me, like this or is she in over her head?

"You sure about this or do you want to watch the movie?" Did I really say that out loud? Jesus Christ, what the fuck is wrong with me? It's like I'm trying to sabotage myself.

She breathes heavy trying to catch her breath. "It's not a glitch, the first storm troopers were clones of Jango Fett; after he died, they shut down the cloning process and started to recruit people for storm trooper duty. That's why they're different heights."

I move my head back and lower my eyebrows. Wait, if she knew this, then she didn't come here to watch the movie. I stare at her for a second, trying to figure out what the hell just happened.

"Yeah, I'm sure." She pulls my lips down to hers.

Three small words and all doubt erases from my mind,

leaving behind animal instincts. I break from her lips and slide my fingers along each side of her panties, slowly pulling them down the soft skin of her legs and tossing them on the floor. She sits up just as I crawl back toward her. Here it is, the moment she stops me and destroys my spirit.

She reaches down to the hem of my shirt and yanks it up and over my head in one swoop. She really does want the whole Vic Steele experience. Hate to break it to her, but nothing that's happening tonight is remotely close to what I'm used to. We're on a whole new playing field tonight, and for once I don't want to fuck it up. She runs her fingers along the ink on my chest to my biceps, slowly moving to my abs and stopping at the button on my jeans. My heart thumps like gasoline runs through my veins. She pulls open the button and shoves her hand down my jeans, grabbing onto every inch of me.

I gasp. A million volts of electricity flow through me, like a bolt of lightning struck me full force. Enough of the teasing, I need her and I need her now. She moves her hands to the rim of my jeans and tugs on them. I dig in my back pocket for my wallet and quickly pull out the condom I always keep in the end slot. I slide down my jeans and boxers in a move I should have patented, and kick them off into oblivion.

She breathes heavy, like she just ran the Boston Marathon. I rip the condom open with my teeth and quickly slide it on. I grip the skirt of her sundress and move it up and over her body, tossing it over my shoulder. Her perfect skin glistens in the dim lighting of my living room. Every inch of her is flawless. I hover over her, slowly lowering myself to meet her lips. She runs her fingertips along my back. Her arms tremble.

She's either filled with adrenaline or things just got real in her brain. Should I stop? Maybe we shouldn't do this tonight. What the fuck am I thinking? It's like some deranged angel infiltrated my brain.

I get it, she's scared. Afraid I'm going to break her in half or something. Every cell in my body wants to fuck her into next week but I'll go for making her beg for more instead. I press myself against her and softly run my lips along hers. She wraps her arms around me tighter, pulling me close. I move slow and steady, easing into her. She gasps as I fill her completely. Her heart vibrates across my chest. I stop for a second, letting her make the next move.

She holds me close, pushing me deeper inside and we match each other's moves, creating a unique rhythm, quickly gaining speed and momentum. I grow rock hard, unable to stop myself from losing all control. I thrust inside her hard and fast.

She lets out a loud moan and grips my hair, pulling it an a million directions as I push deeper insider her. I hold back the urge to explode. She's about to lose it. I hover above her, staring at her face. I need to see the pleasure bursting through her face when she comes. I move forward hard and fast, throbbing inside her. She lets out a moan that could pass as a scream. I watch a wave of ecstasy take over her face. A split second later I explode inside her, collapsing on top of her chest. Our hearts beat fast, in unison with each other.

I bury my head into her shoulder, catching my breath. She loosens the grip on my hair and lets her arms fall onto my sweaty back. I turn my head and catch a glimpse of the TV screen. You've got to be fucking kidding me. Not sure if we rolled over on the remote or timed it perfectly. The scene with the taller-than-normal storm trooper is about to play.

I slowly ease myself out of her. She squirms as if electric impulses still shock her body. I got to keep this from turning into a disaster. Once the blood returns to her brain she might have second thoughts about what just went down. No reason to make her regret being with me before she gets dressed.

I roll over to the side and wrap my arms around her. "Ready

to have your world rocked?" I point toward the TV. Guess it doesn't matter, her Star Wars knowledge surpasses just about anyone's I know.

She looks at the screen and then turns toward me. "I think I just did."

∽

Sunlight blares in through the window, burning through my brain. I slowly open my eyes. Hailey lies beside me, a few stray strands of her hair dancing as she breathes. Her porcelain skin glows in the sun's rays. A relaxed smile plasters on her face, like she's totally content without a care in the world.

Weird, usually I can't wait until a chick gets out of my bed and leaves. Hell, sometimes I flop around the bed like I had ten cups of coffee the night before just to speed up the process. Not this time. Hailey can stay forever and I wouldn't care. Hell, I'd even like it. What the fuck did she do to me? Not sure if I'll come back from this one. Better question, what happens when she wakes up with a clear head? I nibble at my nails and watch her sleep.

Loud knocking resonates through the quiet apartment. Hailey jumps up, her eyes pop open and lock onto mine. She glances around the room, like last night rushed through her brain and brought her back to reality.

I step out of bed and pull on my boxers that lie on the floor. "Be right back. Sam probably locked himself out again." Jesus Christ, my key is on his goddamn keychain. Maybe he's too wasted to put the key in the lock.

Hailey nods, pulling the sheet up to her neck. What's her deal? It's not like we haven't seen each other naked. Now all of a sudden she's embarrassed of that kick-ass body?

I trek to the door, fiddling with the locks and fling it open. A blonde, wearing daisy dukes with the pockets longer than the shorts and a pink tank top stands in the doorway. The blood drains from my face.

"Hey. I left my purse in the kitchen." I step back and she bursts through. Who the hell is she? My brain rewinds back through the last few months. Nope, never seen her in my life.

"Got it." She hurries through the kitchen with a purse that looks more like a wallet in her hand. "Thanks. See ya." She rushes out, leaving a path of destruction behind.

I close the door and stand still, not sure what's about to go down when I face Hailey. The weight of her stare burns through me. How the hell am I supposed to explain this to her? I don't even know what the fuck just happened.

I turn toward the bedroom. She stands in the archway, fully dressed in her black sundress. Her just-got-fucked hair makes her look sexier than hell. She kills me.

She taps her black high-heel on my floor, creating the rhythm of an angry battle cry. "You had me fooled." She shakes her head.

Chills flood through me. I'm fucked and for once I didn't do anything to deserve it. "Listen, I have no idea who she is." I hold up my hands.

She rolls her eyes and marches forward. "Really...well that makes it worse. You can't even remember your conquests." She holds up her hands making quotation marks in the air.

A crimson hue takes over her face. I want to tackle her on my couch. Make her listen to me. Tell her this isn't my fault and since she walked into my shop I haven't been able to get her off my mind. But nothing comes out, I stand, frozen.

"You can forget about me too." She rips open the door and storms out, slamming it so hard it almost flies off the hinges.

What the fuck just happened?

"Sorry, man. I don't check a chick's inventory before she walks out the door." Sam blows air out his cheeks and plops onto the couch. "Rough night for me too, running on no sleep, and the start of a hangover."

Hailey hates my guts, probably wants me dead, and he wants me to feel sorry for him? I run my hands down my face, dragging them down my chin. "Dude, you just fucked things up big-time for me."

He shrugs and leans his head against the back of the couch. "You'll have another chick here by tonight."

"I want her." I don't want some other girl tonight. I want Hailey hanging around my shop and busting my balls with her smart mouth, shoving her hot body in my face, and pulling it away. Letting me run my hands over every inch of her skin and driving me to the brink of insanity. She brings me to my knees and there's not a fucking thing I can do about it. No one can do that to me.

"What? Hell, if she's that good maybe I'll ask her out." He turns his half-open eyes toward me and smirks.

I throw my arm across the couch, giving him a quick shot to the stomach. "Watch it. She's not like that and I'll beat the fuck outta you if you go near her."

He lets out a loud grunt and curls over. "Not cool." He sits up and rubs his weary eyes. "I get it, this chick's got you by the balls. Believe it or not, I've been there." He wrinkles his forehead, like he's trying to read my mind or something. "If you're that into her, you better tell her. You know…if you can get her to speak to you."

I exhale loudly. "She doesn't want anything to do with me…especially now."

He nods. "Yeah, can't blame her." He flashes a smile and gets up off the couch. "I'm hitting the sheets. Listen to me for once, go talk to her. Never know until you try, dude... Holy shit, I think I just wrote a song."

I toss a throw pillow at him. "Go to friggin' sleep."

He moseys into the spare bedroom.

"Sam."

"Yeah."

"Thanks, bro."

He nods and disappears into the hallway. What am I supposed to say to her? She'll believe whatever the hell she wants anyway. It's pretty much a losing battle. Useless waste of my time. Doesn't matter. I gotta give it shot. She could punch me in the face, slam the door shut as soon as she sees me; hell she might not even let me in the building. No matter what, I need her to know that I want her and no one else even comes close. For the first time in my life I don't want anyone but her. And at the very least I need to finish that tattoo, so I can leave my permanent scar on her forever.

∼

"Coming in?" A girl carrying enough books to start her own library struggles to pull open the door.

I jog toward her, quickly holding it open for her. "Yeah... need help?" Jesus, the security here blows. What if I'm some psycho killer? Guess she'd let me right into the dorms, no questions asked. Another smart girl making an idiotic decision. Yeah, I bet every one of them who wakes up next to me mutters that thought under their breath.

She shakes her head. "I've got this." She scurries through the hallway and turns the corner.

I take a deep breath, blowing air out my puffed cheeks. Okay, gained entrance into the building. Step one complete.

Now, if I only had a schematic for the rest of the plan. Hailey's gonna slam the door in my face, no doubt about it. How can I convince her that whatever this is that we have, deserves a shot?

Overthinking like she would isn't gonna give me magical words that will change her mind. I'll just wing it. Live for the moment and take whatever comes my way. Hmm, telling her that might get me punched in the face. Well, won't be the first time a scorned woman wants me left for dead. I've gotta chance it, live on the wild side.

I march up the steps to her room. My heart pounds against my chest like it's going to break free and fly around the room. I nibble my lip, trying to come up with something...anything to say when she swings open the door. My brain goes blank. I got nothing.

I lift my hand but can't muster up enough energy to knock. Come on Vic...get it together. No sense in pussying out when you came this far. I close my eyes and knock on the cold steel door. The lock jiggles and my eyes pop open, ready to face my fate. The door creaks, moving a centimeter a second, like we're in the middle of a slow motion movie. A lock of her hair hangs down, dancing along her shoulder.

Her eyes travel from my black boots, along my ripped jeans and black T-shirt from last year's tattoo convention, to my face. Her gaze locks with mine and instant flames shoot through me. I stick my foot in the door a split second before she tries to slam it shut, stopping it from closing me out.

"Really, Vic. What's that...a move you mastered from the plethora of doors slammed in your face?" She sneers at me, her eyes filled with hell fire.

Pain radiates along my foot. I don't even give a shit if it's broken. I need her to listen...even if it's just for a minute.

"Uh-huh, another one of my moves." What the fuck...it's like my brain is on man-whore mode. "I'm kidding. I wanted to talk to you."

"I think you said enough this morning...or that girl summed it all up for you." She pushes on the door, trying to wedge my foot from the door jam.

She'll have to cut it off before I leave. "It's not what you think. She was my brother Sam's conquest...not mine."

She shrugs. "Doesn't matter, yours was probably next in line."

"It's not like that...not anymore."

She's not getting it. She somehow de-whoreized me without my consent. Does she think I want to be here groveling and begging for her to spend another minute with me?

"Really...were you visited by three ghosts or something?" Her eyes shimmer, reflecting silver specs of light from the dim hallway. Her knuckles turn white from the death grip she's got on the doorknob.

Even when she's ready to kill she's beautiful. "Something like that. Listen...can we start over?" I run a hand through my hair and lean against the doorjamb.

She lets out a deep breath and shakes her head. "What's the point? You want a friend with benefits...or whatever they call it now."

I lean forward, jolted by the scent of her fruity perfume. "No. I want you."

She loosens her grip on the knob, releasing the pressure on my foot. "Yeah, for now." She exhales loudly and takes a step back. "Then what happens?"

I shrug and let out the breath I didn't realize I'd been holding. "Wish I knew...I can't get you off of mind...ever. I stare at the door of my shop every time it opens hoping it's you, I went on a real date the first time since my high school prom just to be with you. Hell, I'm ready to hire security to stand outside this damn dorm so some psycho doesn't break in."

Her scrunched eyebrows relax and she drops her hand. A small smile forms. "Like some crazy guy sticking his foot in my door?"

"Pretty much." I nod. "Look, I know there's a million reasons going through your head on why I'm the last guy in the world you should be with." I push the door forward and take a few steps into her room. "But it only takes one to change it all...right?"

Her mouth falls open but no words come out.

I push the door closed with my foot and run my hands along her soft cheeks, pressing my forehead against hers. "I guess it's like tattooing, if the color saturation isn't right, it fades with time. Skill helps but when you find that magic combination of perfect skin and ink placed just right the image lasts forever. Like the first time you ever laid your eyes on it... Every time I look at you it's like staring at first ink, perfect in every way."

I close my eyes and swallow hard. "I can't stop thinking about you. I want you...no one else, and it scares the hell out of me." I slowly open my eyes, staring into hers. "I don't know what will happen tomorrow, or next week, or when we're both in Miami but I know that no one else in the world refers to me as an anti-sematic dictator, or spends hours in my shop bad-mouthing my work and demanding a tattoo they're not sure they can handle, or can bring me to my knees with one look."

She locks her eyes with mine and wraps her arms around me. "Shut up." She slams her lips against mine, her body trembles.

"One more thing." I suck on her bottom lip as I pull away. "We're finishing that tattoo. No way Vic Steele's girl is walking around with an unfinished piece."

She lowers an eyebrow. "You're not afraid I'm going to pass out in your chair?"

"I'm kinda hoping you do." I wink.

"Ah, there's the Vic Steele I know." She presses her lips against mine.

Nah, that guy's long gone, but this one's ready for a wild ride, wherever it takes us.

ABOUT THE AUTHOR

Romance author by night, pharmacist by day, Amy Gale loves rock music and the feel of sand between her toes. She attended Wilkes University where she graduated with a Doctor of Pharmacy degree. In addition to writing, she enjoys baking, scary movies, rock concerts, and reading books at the beach. She lives in the lush forest of Northeastern Pennsylvania with her husband, six cats, and golden retriever.

For more information
www.authoramygale.com
amzie13793@aol.com

Made in the USA
Middletown, DE
22 July 2025